GIMLET EYE GUNN

H. BEDFORD-JONES

# GIMLET EYE GUNN

## H. BEDFORD-JONES

### COVER ILLUSTRATION BY

### LEE BROWN COYE

ALTUS PRESS • 2016

© 2016 Altus Press • First Edition—2016

PUBLISHING HISTORY

"Gimlet Eye Gunn" originally appeared in the March 25, 1945 issue of *Short Stories* magazine (Vol. 190, No. 6).

THANKS TO

Rebecca Burns and Gerd Pircher

# TABLE OF CONTENTS

CHAPTER ONE

I T   I S   all right to tell this yarn as it is long after the war, it may be made a bit more credible to the average person. Even now, admittedly, it is more than a trifle staggering, even though well vouched for. Since it is not a war story, however, and does not have to be written to get past the censor, suppose we take a gander at it.

Larsen came to this country from Norway at five years of age, was eighteen when he got into the war, and was twenty-one when he started to invade the Philippines with MacArthur, though MacArthur was not aware of it, because Larsen was only the tail-gunner in a bomber that went haywire.

The reason she went haywire that afternoon was that she caught a terrific dose of flak. This was in the hot naval business outside Leyte. When the communications went dead, Larsen knew the worst must have happened, and it had. He had been washed out as a pilot before going into gunnery, and knew his way around a bit, but when he made his way forward he was appalled. She had taken everything there was to take, apparently, and he waded through a bloody mess that left him reeling. He was the only soul alive.

By the time he had pulled what remained of the pilot and co-pilot off the controls he was shaken and trembly, and no wonder. The ship was going like a bat out of hell, but in a fluttery sort of way that showed she would not hold together long; she was at five thousand feet, luckily, but was losing altitude,

with wings and fuselage ripped all to hell 'n' gone. The radio
was dead. When he discovered this, Larsen looked around to
see where he was; but he had been going five miles a minute
and there was nothing in sight. He stared down blankly, with
a sense of panic. Leyte gone—the smoke of the burning carrier
gone—everything gone!

Dripping blood over the sea, the bomber flew on with Larsen
paralyzed at the controls. The sea-surface told him he was
gradually dropping, but the instruments were dead like everything else on board. Larsen had on his parachute and might
have taken to it and a rubber boat in case of fire, but there was
no fire, and he had heard a lot about sharks. He stayed where
he was and hoped against hope, straining his eyes at the horizon.

Then, off to the south—at least, he thought from the sun
that it must be south, though it was not—he saw a blue land
loom, and frantically headed the bomber for it. He cut down
the engines, and a good thing he did, for the wings were shaking
to pieces. Also, he got his parachute and other essentials ready;
it looked like he might have to jump at any instant, to judge by
the vibration. His pockets were crammed with cigarettes and
chocolate bars and other stuff he had taken aboard at the last
minute and had not touched, but he dared not try to get rid of
the weight now. Besides, he might need it all.

The dying bomber thundered onward, alone in the empty
sky. The blue shadow grew against the sea-edge like a gob of
goo on a bayonet, but he knew he was not going to make it,
because the shimmering waves below were coming close. The
bombs! They were still in the bay. He found the electric release
and pressed the button. He could feel the upward thrust at once,
as the doors opened and the bombs fell away, but he did not
look back. He had picked up something else, dead ahead.

This was an island, a small one with two peaks sticking up
out of the water, well this side of the blue coast beyond. He
came closer; there was nothing to the patch of island except
the two peaks and a depression between them, but it was a
lifesaver. The peaks could not be more than a few hundred feet

high—he was not above them, but on a level with them. But he could see a fringing reef, and it looked ugly as the surf broke over it.

Then his heart skipped a beat, as the sea reached up and clutched at him—almost down! Desperately, he set the gyro pilot and it took hold. He scrambled aft. The bomb bay was still open; he dumped out corpses, ammunition cans, anything he could find. The ship rose a little, but she was not going to make the island.

Like everyone in the service, he had received a thorough course in ditching drill, but drill was far different from the present circumstances; and he did not intend to wait till the bomber struck. As he inflated his Mae West, he eyed the shoreline inside the wide lagoon formed by the reef. He wanted to get out before she hit, and there was no need of a parachute now; he had just time to shed it.

The line of reef was rushing at him; she was barely going to clear it. Already the waves were lapping up at her. He opened the hatch and stood ready. She was over the reef and past it, fuselage right on the water—then he pulled the dinghy release and jumped, a bare instant before she struck her tail and plunged under in a huge shower of spray.

THE DINGHY inflated itself, and when he came clear, the rubber craft was floating at a little distance. He swam to it and did not try to get aboard; he just hung on and kicked, and the white beach came close. All sign of the bomber had vanished.

Before he knew it, Larsen touched bottom and came crawling out to the white sand, where a thousand sandfleas went jumping and skipping in all directions. He pulled the rubber doughnut up after him, then staggered on toward the trees, and went to pieces in total collapse, and dropped.

It had been early morning when he got here. He did not waken until well along in the afternoon. He blinked, sat up, and stared around, bewildered.

Everything came back to him of itself. There was nothing to suggest it in sight except the rubber boat on the sand. Not a trace of the bomber. He sat for a while staring frowningly at the water, then looked around. He got out of his flying clothes, now dry, found a cigarette packet, and in the center located a

smoke that was not brown and ruined, and got it alight, spreading out the others on the sand. He emptied his pockets and looked at his watch. Not watertight, it had stopped; he set it by guess at four o'clock.

The cigarette gone, he got up and went to the dinghy. The compartments were stocked with rations and needfuls; cigarettes, too, thank Uncle Sam! He got everything out and hid the packets under the trees, then went back and stared at the white coral sand. Someone else was or had been here, for the marks were plain. Except in stories and wet sand, footprints do not show up as such; he could make nothing of these, and went to the creek. Here he drank long and thirstily.

"No reception party on hand," he observed aloud, and squinted up at the two small peaks. These were of bare rock, but below them trees were thick. Shouting, he gained no response, so he started up the creek by a well-traveled path that appeared.

Within a few hundred feet, he was looking around in utter amazement. He came upon a big canoe, helpless for use, with a huge hole in its bottom. Pigs ran about wild, and quite a few chickens were in sight, less wild. Over across the creek showed patches of cultivated ground. And on ahead was a collection of houses beside the stream. Houses! Sure enough, there was no mistake. He came close, staring at them. Native houses thatched with nipa.

He hurried to them, calling. No answer came. He looked into one after another; all were empty and deserted, empty of

people, empty of effects. Yet they had not been very long abandoned, by the looks. The taro and yam patches were clear of
grass or weeds; a pile of camotes, the island yams, lay freshly
dug.

Larsen almost forgot his providential escape in the contem-
plation of this mystery. No people anywhere, yet no sign of
death or disease. No boats except the one busted craft. The
natives had not dropped everything and fled upon his arrival;
there was not so much as a sleeping mat in the houses.

"Be damned if I can savvy it!" He came into the open, peering
at the trees, at the creek, and lit another smoke. The sound of
his own voice was good to hear. "Where's everybody? Why have
they skipped out? Tell me that, will you?"

He jumped. There was a cackle of human laughter.

"They were scared of old Gunner Gunn, that's why!" came
the words.

Larsen swung around. Nothing in sight, no one anywhere.

"Hey, there!" he called. "Where are you? Come on, show
yourself! I'm a friend! Are you English or American? Come on
out of hiding! I won't hurt you! Amigos!"

Another faint cackling laugh responded and then was stilled.
Larsen called, threatened, cajoled, and the only response was
silence.

Dazedly, he made his way back to the beach where he had
landed. Somebody was assuredly hanging around; it was a
human voice that had answered his query, and it had spoken
good English. Mystery, sure enough!

However, sunset was approaching, and being a very practical
young man, Larsen resolved to let the mystery take care of itself
for the moment. He wanted a dip in the lagoon, and he was
hungry. So he stripped and had a plunge, then attacked his
cache of rations. He had food and water and shelter, and the
rest could wait till morning. His cigarettes were drying, and he
stretched out comfortably in the warm sand as the stars began
to dot the greenish sky.

He lay awake a long while. Where this island was, he had no idea. Tomorrow, he reflected, he would explore the place. It was a small island; he would have no difficulty in running down that voice of mystery. It did not come from an enemy, or he would have been attacked before this. Might have been a parrot or a mynah bird, of course; but the voice had been very human.

LULLED BY the surf vibrations from the reefs, he drifted off to sleep before he knew it.

Warm sunlight wakened him; he was on the eastern side of the islet, obviously. He rose, stretched luxuriously, rid of the baggy flying suit, and went down to the creek to douse his head. He came back and attacked his rations anew—it was a K-ration he had opened and there were two others in their waxed containers.

He was eating away heartily when he became vaguely aware of something wrong. At first he could not place what it was; then he woke up. The rubber boat was gone! Yet he had pulled it up far above high water mark.

"Damn!" he said, and went to investigate, without result. The dry sand was scuffed up; the tide was low, and there were no footprints in the wet sand. "Damn!" he repeated, and stood looking around angrily. He lifted his voice.

"Whoever you are, bring that boat back or you'll pay for it! Hear me?"

Only the surf answered him. This was silly business, he thought, addressing the blank trees. Well, he would soon attend to the blighter! He went back and finished his meal, rather soberly. Whoever had taken the boat, could have killed him in his sleep had it been an enemy; this obvious reflection was distinctly annoying. He had no weapon of any kind except a pocket-knife and a razor, part of the toilet kit in the boat.

He palmed his long, lean features, took the razor and went to the creek. There he made shift to get a shave, of sorts; might have been better, but he was in a hurry. He wanted to settle this disturbing business without delay. He looked out at the lagoon where the wrecked bomber lay hidden, and for almost the first time it occurred to him that he was alive where he might well have been dead.

With a somewhat stealthy glance around, Larsen came down on one knee and repeated the Lord's Prayer, the only one he could bring to mind.

"…world without end, Amen. And thanks, God," he concluded, then rose. It made him feel better, somehow, though he was not much for religion. And now, hiding his stuff away once more, he started for the deserted village. There were paths everywhere.

CHAPTER TWO

THE ISLAND consisted of nothing more than the two little rocky peaks, with the creek and depression between them, where stood the village. The stream came from springs in the north peak, as Larsen later discovered. Here in the valley, where there were no clearings the vegetation was super thick, but was cut up by trails, evidently lately used.

Larsen picked a trail at random, careless whether it led to the western shore of the island or elsewhere. It proved to pierce the jungle in the direction of the south peak, lower than the other and very close to the village. Indeed, before half an hour he found himself clear of brush and on the rocky hummock itself. Also, the trail was deeply worn and must lead somewhere, he reflected.

He was halfway up when he came to a halt, gazing out over the southward sea that glittered in the new sunlight. All empty, but he remembered the blue loom of land to the westward. He could get a sight of it from the crest of the peak—

"Ho. You're on the right track!" cackled a voice. The same voice he had heard the previous evening. He jumped, swung around, saw nothing.

"Who the devil are you? Come out and show yourself!" he called.

"You'll see me soon enough, lad," came the reply. "Who am I? Weston Gunn himself. Gimlet Eye they called me, because I could lay a gun better than the best of 'em; a damned fine gunner, too. There's not much of me left to prove it, but I was broad in the beam and thick in the tail, with a big foot and a strong hand and an eye for the wenches. You wouldn't think it to look at me now."

The voice was real. Larsen tried to follow it, but could see nothing of the speaker. He examined the hummock of rock closely. It was pitted with holes—caves, by looks of them.

He could make no particular sense of the words, but it did not occur to him to feel any fear.

"Are you the guy that stole my rubber boat?" he demanded.

"Aye, that was old Gimlet Eye himself," responded another cackle of mirth. "Go make a song for Gunner Gunn, his day is o'er, his race is run! Zanzibar was my fishing grounds, lad, but I came to Makassar and looted the pearls. That was just two hundred years ago, and here I be today, sitting, looking out to sea for the ship that comes no more—me in my fine scarlet coat wi' the gold braid. All tarnished it is now."

Two hundred years ago—what the hell!

"What kind of a joke are you trying to get off?" demanded Larsen hotly. "Come into the open, you damned fool! I won't hurt you!"

"You'd better not, my lad," was the response. "Keep following your nose and it'll bring you to me. Poor Jim North, he was the bosun's mate, he was put in the cave with me, but he ain't there now. I couldn't find him. King Kaiwas was king of Tiger Island in those days; a Malay, and paid with diamonds, and I was at sea for him. Many a Jap I killed then, and many another will I kill before long, so watch out sharp."

"Where's everybody?" sang out Larsen. "What's become of the natives here?"

"Scared of me. I scared 'em off. There were some Japs here, but I killed 'em. You will find their bones at the west landing, behind the old ship's ribs. Ho! It takes old Gimlet Eye to kill Japs! I wish I had the guns out of your ship that's under the lagoon—I'd show you how to use 'em!"

"Be damned to you. I'm a gunner myself," said Larsen, then checked his words with a silly sense of futility. A laugh responded and died away. Nothing else came; Gunner Gunn had departed, apparently.

Now, at the moment all this wild talk—for it seemed wild—sounded like the ravings of a maniac to Larsen, and small blame to him.

He stood reflectively. Here, he thought, must be some poor devil of a lunatic who imagined himself in the guise of an ancient freebooter or pirate seaman—and talked like it to boot. This was the obvious conclusion, yet in some ways it hardly made good sense at that. The natives, for instance, would have known him for a lunatic and would not have deserted their island home because of his ravings. Apparently the fellow was harmless enough and meant no deviltry.

Weston Gunn—old Gimlet Eye—Gunner Gunn! A funny business, certainly.

Larsen went on. The path was easy to negotiate, and curved upward, around the rise of the peak. It brought him at length to the west side of the hummock, which here fell down in long rocky descents to brush and trees and the west shore of the islet. But it was not at the shore that he stood gazing.

Westward lay the land he had seen from aloft, long and high and blue; about twenty miles away, he figured roughly. And something else—the triangular sail of a native boat, apparently heading for this island. He gazed at it, wishing he had binoculars. It was no more than three or four miles away, apparently, and seemed headed straight in.

He almost turned back there; it was in his mind to go down to the valley and seek the west side of the island. If that boat held natives, they would take him off. Good! However, he determined to go ahead and reach the summit, or wherever the path might lead, for it certainly went somewhere. If that boat did not take him off, he reflected, he might fetch some brush and wood up the peak and prepare a beacon as a signal. No rush about getting down. The wind was light and that boat would not be in for a long while—if it were coming in. It might only be on a tack.

So he went ahead.

He did not have far to go. Short of the summit, the path swerved and brought him to a level expanse, a shelf backed by the tip of the peak; there were more pitted caves here. And there was something else. Something that fetched him to a halt and held him bug-eyed, incredulous, the flesh prickling up his spine.

For here, seated on a pile of rock against the cliff, the wind streaming out his fluttering garments, sat Gimlet Eye himself. He knew instantly why those natives had been scared off the islands. He was scared stiff himself, for a moment.

The Thing sat there, one boot cocked up atop a rounded, rusty old sea-chest, pistol in one hand, cutlass in the other. A Thing draped in tattered garments, long gray beard framing the white glint of teeth, blue eyes staring at the sky from a skeleton face. It was monstrous, inhuman, shocking. The way those wrists and hands hung down, clutching the weapons, the way those eyes peered out at heaven and sea, appalled him. He could fancy a wreath of smoke curling up from the pistol.

Larsen hung on to himself; he was not easily shaken, but there was something outside of all his experience. Terrible thoughts shook him. Was it possible that he had heard a ghostly voice, and not a living man? Had the ghost of Gunner Gunn been speaking to him?

"Maybe I'm going nuts," he said, anxious for the sound of his own voice.

Was the Thing real? It was! Horrible real, yet he doubted his own senses, quite pardonably. He spoke again, to convince himself he was awake.

"Hey, you! Are you Gunner Gunn? If you are, speak up!"

He almost took an answer for granted, after that talk with nothing down the trail, but none came. The Thing peered up at the empty skies, unmoving, unspeaking.

"Of course it won't speak. It's dead," said Larsen. "Been dead two hundred years, too—if that blasted voice told the truth."

He moved closer, close enough to touch the Thing. It was real and it was dead, plenty dead. It was a combination of skeleton and mummy. Larsen had the answer from the holes in the rock behind—a squeaking and rustling. He knew what that meant; bats. Those caves in the cliff were filled with bats.

Now the Thing began to make sense to him. Somebody, whether old Gimlet Eye in the flesh or not, had been laid to rest in one of those caves a long time ago. To judge from the size and contour of that pistol, it had been plenty long ago. Had the corpse moved out here of itself? Not likely.

He came close, touched the mummified hands, and examined critically. A skeleton does not hang together by itself, nor does a mummified corpse hold on to the weapons by itself. Looking carefully, he found what he sought. Bits of wire held the weapons in those dead and awful hands. And the blue eyes in the eye-sockets of the skull—ha! Bits of bright blue glass fixed in place, with a damned glitter shining through them!

Larsen stepped back and fumbled for a cigarette, with a surge of untold relief.

"Well, I'll be damned! This is something, sure enough!" he said, addressing the silent shape. "What's in that chest—anything? You poor old skinny coot, you sure look like hell, and I mean hell, too! Somebody sure did a work of art when they put you together and stacked you out here; but who did it?"

No reply. The ghost had ceased to speak, or was elsewhere.

Ghost? Larsen shook his head. He took no stock in the supernatural—but he did have a slightly creepy feeling at the remembrance of the voice, and what it had said. Weston Gunn himself speaking? Maybe, maybe not. It had told him what he would find here though, and it had done him no harm—but it had stolen the rubber boat. And spirits do not monkey with material things. So that ruled out spirits.

Larsen got a smoke alight and squinted at Gunner Gunn critically.

"Somebody wired you up and put you here and scared hell out of the natives—that much is clear enough," he ruminated. "But the voice that spoke to me! Either somebody was kidding me or a lunatic is running around loose, or else it was your ghost. And I'm betting it was no ghost."

He eyed the holes in the rock with no ambition whatever to explore them. Stuck away in those caves, probably high and dry inside at all weathers, a corpse might very well mummify. He went close to the figure and eyed the chest curiously. A glint of greenish corroded brass caught his eye at one end. Initials could be descried, outlined with brass nails or tacks—W. G. Weston Gunn? Maybe. And the tattered garments, falling to pieces, that hung on the corpse—it did look like a scarlet coat, sure enough. Larsen gazed at the faceless skull and shivered, then reality asserted itself and he laughed.

The mystery was dispelled, in large part. Somebody had found this mummy lying in a cave and had fixed it up like this; with it had been documents, probably, giving the story about Gimlet Eye Gunn. The same Somebody had apparently picked up enough from them to imagine himself Mr. Gunn—since it was not very likely that he would be playing a joke. It was all more like the work of a lunatic. Only....

"Only, somehow, what the voice said sounded real as hell," thought Larsen a trifle uncomfortably. "And be damned if the eyes in that skull don't look to be alive! I don't like it, any of it, but I'm not falling for any ghost stuff, and I'm not falling for old whiskers yonder either! So long, mister, and be good."

He started away, recollecting that boat he had seen and making for the point on the trail that would open out the western view. If that boat were really coming to the island, he wanted to be down at the shore when it came.

Oh, boy! It was coming in, sure enough—not more than a couple of miles out now, he figured, and pointing steadily in. He could see dots of figures aboard, and even a flutter of white in the stern.

"Mrs. Gunn, maybe" he thought, striding down the trail, and a laugh came to his lips. "What did that screwball say about the bones of Japs at the western beach? Back of a ship's ribs. Huh! We'll see about that."

His pace quickened. To be honest about it, he was just as glad to get away from old Gimlet Eye Gunn and his rusted chest and his pistol, with that foot cocked up on the chest as large as life—ugh!

## CHAPTER THREE

TWICE, ON his way down to the creek below, Larsen addressed the empty air loudly, expecting to hear the cackling laugh and the husky voice of Mr. Gunn, but only silence made response.

He hurried, though not from fear. The morning was splendidly warm and brilliant; when he got down to the windless little valley and the creek, he was sweating. He turned westward by a heavily worn trail, and the creek lessened, then disappeared.

To the western shore could not have been more than a mile, but so thick was the vegetation of tree and shrub that not even a sight of the sea was visible. The trail continued hard-beaten and wide, as though much used, but there was no further indication of any habitation. Of the little north peak he could see only that bare rock stuck up above the trees, but it was steeper than the other and its base seemed to form the north side of the island. Nothing much here except the one tiny valley and its village.

Suddenly the vegetation thinned to thorny pandanus scrub and he stood looking down at the beach and the sea beyond. The beach was white coral sand like the eastern one and made a curving cove, a few hundred feet wide. The water was thirty feet from him, and there, sure enough, was coming the boat!

Larsen goggled at it excitedly. A quarter-mile out, it was obviously headed for the cove and beach; he stood motionless, not daring to come out into the open as yet, lest he frighten the craft off. In the prow, the figures of natives were visible, brown men wearing bright-hued sarongs, Malays or Dyaks; the patch of white in the stern was not visible now. Probably a big fishing craft, he thought, and wondered if any of them would savvy English.

Then, closer at hand, he saw something else that jerked at him.

Out of the white sand, buried to the eyes, protruded the skeleton bow and ribs of a small ship. It was pointing seaward, so that he could look slap into what had been the slanting fore deck and was now drifted sand. "Behind the old ship's ribs" had said that ghostly voice. And sure enough, there they were—at least, he could see a pile of bones and several skulls heaped in the very bows, sand over and around them. Japs? Dead Japs piled there to decay in the sunlight? Hard to say. They were human bones, at any rate. What gave Larsen a queer turn was this corroboration of what the Voice had said to him.

"Next thing you know, I'll be dreaming about that screwball," muttered Larsen with a growl.

The boat was coming in fast; he turned to it in relief. This was real and tangible at all events. He heard the voices of the Malays as they brought down the sail and put out sweeps. He could see their flat, dish-like faces and their black teeth. They looked over their shoulders at the island, as though in fear. Ha! Perhaps they were some of the natives who had been scared off! Larsen stood motionless.

Then, close inshore, the boat began to turn. There was no surf here; it was no doubt broken by reefs far out. He watched, in swift alarm; turning around? No. Only to back in, stern first. This was odd, certainly....

His thoughts died away. His jaw fell. A white-clad figure stood up in the stern as it came in upon the sand—a white woman, by the Lord! He saw her jump out, and saw bundles tossed after her. She caught them, laughing, and he heard her voice say something to the brown men in their own tongue.

Then, abruptly he came alive. Two of the Malays were at the sail, hoisting it. Two others stood up, handling their oars like poles to push off. They were going back—they were leaving! With a sudden wild yell, Larsen leaped out of the brush and went across the sand at a plunging run.

"Hold on! Hold on!" he shouted.

A yell arose from the brown men—fear unmistakable. The sail jerked up, the oars were put out again, and the rowers dug in. The boat leaped away from the shore, and went like mad. Larsen, shouting and swearing in mingled fury and dismay, came to a halt at the beach, regardless of the woman in white. The more he shouted and shook his fist, the faster went the boat, slanting over to the wind, speeding out like a skimming bird.

"No use," said the woman. "They're too scared of the place already to wait. I had to bribe them heavily to land here."

LARSEN SWUNG around to her, almost with a groan. It was checked at once. He saw a young woman, smiling: a healthily tanned, undeniably pleasant-looking young woman, wearing the tattered and much mended and patched remains of a nurse's uniform. Surprise came into her face as she met his gaze.

"Hello!" she exclaimed. "You're not Dr. Bowe!"

"Eh? Hell, no," said Larsen. "He's on the phone in the other office. Say, what does all this mean? Am I clear off my nut?"

"Apparently you are," she replied calmly, watching him. "You certainly give every indication of it."

"Ouch!" he said, and drew a long breath. The boat was gone, far gone. Yet he could only stare helplessly at the young woman. "Say, are you an American girl?"

"My mother always told me so, and I believed her," said she, and cut loose with a twinkling smile. They looked at each other for a moment; under her twinkle, Larsen lost his sulky amazement and broke into a laugh. He was good to see when he laughed, for his features, usually too serious, rippled into mirth and strength and quick appeal.

"Sorry, sister," he said, and extended his hand. "My name's Pete Larsen. Air Force gunner. You'll have to excuse my symptoms, because I don't know where I am and seeing you was certainly a jolt. Our bomber went down on the other side of the island and I got ashore, and that may explain a lot of things."

"Well, it explains you anyhow," she said frankly, and shook hands. "I'm Susan Mason, originally of Des Moines, Iowa, and more lately from the mission hospital at Cuyacan, and the concentration camp over yonder at Baguio Island—that's the blue mass overlooking the horizon. Now can we get out of the sun and talk comfortably? I don't suppose you're alone here?"

"Yep. Except for Gimlet Eye Gunn—and I don't know yet whether he's a ghost or a skeleton or a mental case worse off than I am," rejoined Larsen. "Let's have your luggage and we'll hunt the shade yonder."

"Be careful," she said, as he stooped to gather up the bundles. "Those are grub and clothes and personal possessions, all I have in the world."

"I'm not that hungry," he said, and led the way toward the sand-gulfed ship, whose high prow cast a triangle of shade across the sand.

Here they settled themselves comfortably. Larsen produced cigarettes and at her quick exclamation of delight passed her one and held a light.

"I'll lead off, Susie, unless you want to start first."

"No, go ahead. There's so much I don't know! Until lately, I've been a prisoner ever since the war started."

"You poor kid! All right, then—"

He told how he had come here, and sketched the background of events that had brought him here. She listened intently, dragging at the cigarette in avid enjoyment. Only native tobacco and little of that, said she, for a long while. When he had finished, with no mention as yet of Gunner Gunn, she nodded.

"I begin to get it, Pete," she said, with a sigh. "We've heard rumors, of course, and once or twice have seen planes, that's all. Well, everybody in these parts was concentrated over there on Baguio Island—that means Windy Island. It's northeast of Zamboanga, and a long way from Leyte. Last month we had a chance to get away and some of us took it. We've been hiding out with the natives in the mountains, ever since.

"Then I heard that Dr. Bowe had come over here; this is called Tiger Island. Why, what's the matter?" she exclaimed at his startled word. He waved his hand.

"Never mind. Tell you later. No tiger's been seen around here, thank heaven!"

"Oh, it's an old name, I suppose. Well, things were pretty tough for us and I thought I'd come here and find Dr. Bowe. He was our head surgeon and a splendid man. The natives said nobody lived here any more because devils had driven them out, and after a lot of talk they agreed to bring me, and here I am."

Larsen looked at her. "What you want to find this doctor for? You folks in love?"

A gasp and a laugh escaped her. "Heavens, no! He has a family back home. You're a terribly direct sort of person, aren't you?"

"I dunno," replied Larsen. "I was never much good at beating around the bush. I wouldn't blame him at that. You're a knock-out."

Her lips twitched. "Thanks, Pete. I need to find him because I've got a bad appendix and it must come out, and nobody else could do it. I pretty near passed out a couple of weeks ago, and another attack may finish me if the appendix bursts. Any more secrets you'd like to know?"

LARSEN CONSIDERED her reflectively and nodded.

"Yeah, several; but let 'em pass. I was curious, that's all. Didn't mean any harm, Susie. Well, I have bad news for you. Your doc isn't here. The place is deserted—and not deserted enough."

"What was it you said about a ghost?"

"Well, suppose we let that wait a bit. I'd like to see what happens; if you hear what I hear and so forth. I'm not sure if I've been having delusions or what."

"You seem remarkably sane to me, all kidding aside," she observed.

He grinned. "Hope it's true. Any chance of your natives coming back with the boat?"

"No, I'm sorry to say. You saw how they skipped out."

"Okay. Then let's go and I'll show you around my domain. I'm not sure who's king of Tiger island, me or Gimlet Eye; but I haven't seen a living soul since I got here, so you're safe from Japs, anyhow. Want to be moving?"

She nodded. They rose, and Larsen picked up the bundles, refusing to let her help. He took occasion to fling a glance in through the gaunt ribs of the wreck, and saw the bones and skulls, several of the latter. He grunted and said nothing, but led the way to the path that traversed the little valley.

"Some good-looking native shacks over ahead," he said. "And plenty of grub in sight—pigs and chickens and yams and so forth. I expect there are fish, too. I've got hooks and line that came with the rubber boat."

"Oh! You have a rubber boat?"

"Well, I had. It vanished on me the first night—hell! That was only last night. Seems like I've been here a week," he admitted awkwardly. "I got here yesterday morning and slept until late in the afternoon; mixed me up a bit."

She laughed, and he struck out ahead of her to avoid further questions.

In due time the trail picked up the creek and the dozen or more houses of the village came into sight. These they examined minutely, and finally picked on two small ones, side by side, for occupancy. Susan Mason stored her bundles in one.

"What stuff I've got is hidden down by the shore," said Larsen. "Come on and we'll get it, and I'll show you the lagoon where my ship went down. Say, I'm tickled pink to have you here, Susie! Anything human would be a relief."

"Backhanded but still a compliment," said she cheerfully. "It's sure plenty warm under these trees, Pete! I could do with a dip in the creek, too, or a swim if the shore waters are safe from sharks. This is like being clear out of the whole world!"

He gave her a look. "If I were you I wouldn't count on too much privacy around here, Susie gal. Maybe looks are deceptive."

"Why, what do you mean?"

He paid no heed to the question, but led the way toward the beach. The stretch of white sand came in sight, and then he halted abruptly.

"That's what I mean," he said, as he caught the cackling laugh of Mr. Gunn.

## CHAPTER FOUR

"HO-HO-HO! YOU have a good eye for a wench, lad, same as old Gimlet Eye!" rang out the voice.

Larsen turned and met her eyes. "Do you hear it?"

"Why, yes, of course!"

"Oh! That's fine." He drew a long breath of relief, and looked around. Nothing in sight. He raised his voice. "Hello there, Gimlet Eye! Come out and meet the lady."

"Hell's bells and a sack o' barley!" came an instant response. "I was never a rogue for the ladies. Give old Gunner Gunn a wench who can kiss a tankard and wipe out a gun with a wet mop. None of your fine mincing ladies. Be damned to them all—"

A stormy lusty volley of oaths resounded. Susan Mason eyed Larsen critically then stared around.

"You're not a ventriloquist, by any chance?" she inquired. "No, I see it's not you. Who is it?"

"Ask me something easy," said Larsen. "Hey, Gimlet Eye! I saw your hunk of bones up on the hill. What's in the chest?"

"Look and see, you blasted rogue," came the reply, apparently from the trees. "I'm going fishing for a gun from your ship one of these nights. I ever fancied a Long Tom and had a neat one I got out of a Bristol ship, but she was a hard old girl to fire. I've been talking with one of your crew, a bloody fine chap named Dierschow, and he's showing me how to work your guns. Take your wench up the hill and show her my bones, but mind you don't touch 'em or I'll haunt you."

Larsen gulped and felt prickles run up his spine. Dierschow! Walter Dierschow had been bombardier and navigator of the ship—how in the devil's name could this voice know it? He looked at Susan.

"Did you hear that? Dierschow?"

"Of course, I did," she said. "Why shouldn't I?"

"Damn it, I don't know—Walter Dierschow was our navigator." Sweat started from his cheeks, he stared around desperately. "I don't know what to make of this—ghosts don't talk or fire guns."

"Ease off, soldier," she said quietly. "Don't let it get your nerves. There'll be a very ordinary explanation, be sure of that."

"Yes, you talk like a blasted hospital nurse," he broke out. "How can there be any explanation of his knowing that name?"

The cackle of Mr. Gunn's laughter sounded, then thinned away and died. Evidently Gimlet Eye found Larsen's bewilderment very amusing.

"I'm sorry, Susie," said Larsen after a minute. "It gave me a bad turn, for a fact. See here, suppose we go up the hill and I'll show you old Gunn, and you'll savvy the whole thing—as far as I do, anyhow."

"Good idea. I'll let the swim wait," said she. "Then we'll come back down and start housekeeping, eh?"

"Okay. Say!" he exclaimed suddenly. "That voice—was that your Doctor Bowe?"

"It certainly was not," she replied. "He has a low, soft, gentle voice, and he never did any cursing and swearing. But see here—do you mean to tell me this was just a voice? Why, that's impossible, Pete!"

"That's what I thought," he rejoined. "And he stole my rubber boat, too. Ghosts don't do things like that. If it wasn't a ghost and wasn't a delusion, then what was it?"

"A man, of course," she said with a sniff.

"All right. Come along and I'll show you the man, old Gunn himself."

H E  L E D  the way, found the path going up the hill, and kept going in advance. They reached the shelf at last where Gimlet Eye sat in all his glory, and Susan examined him absorbedly, while Larsen examined her with equal attention. She was certainly worth it, he decided; he liked her bright, cheery way and her lithe suppleness, and in fact everything about her. She wore native sandals, probably for lack of shoes, and the old mended nurse's uniform was a shapeless bag—that is, if anything could be shapeless when draped on her.

"I might swap clothes with Mr. Gunn," said she. "We're both scarecrows. What's in that chest?"

"Search me. I was wondering myself." Larsen came to life. "You hold up his foot and I'll move the chest out."

She complied. The old and rusted chest slid out and Larsen managed to pry up the curved top lid. There was nothing inside. He closed it again and shoved it back under the booted, skeleton foot.

"Look here!" Susan was unashamedly examining Mr. Gunn's anatomy. "Part of him is mummy, part skeleton. And the bones have been wired together. Expertly. I'll bet a doctor did it. Probably Dr. Bowe."

"You'd better not carry your post-mortem too far," warned Larsen. "You heard what he said. He'll sure as hell haunt you, Susie."

She gave over her examination and joined him, sitting on a bit of rock and looking at the cliffs. He explained his theory about the cave, and she nodded, an attractive little frown wrinkling her forehead.

"Why is it," said Larsen, "that wrinkles look like the deuce on an old woman, and make a young one look mighty pleasant?"

"They lend a bit of dignity." Laughing, she turned to him. "You can't figure out any answer to this thing—the voice and all?"

"Nope. Can you?"

"Not a trace of one. I like those blue eyes of his, don't you? They seem lifelike. And this is a grand place for a lookout!"

She sat gazing over the farflung waters, until she became aware of Larsen's fixed regard, and stood up.

"Want to go? If we—oh!"

She swung around, startled, at a clanging crash from behind her. The cutlass had escaped from the fingers of Mr. Gunn and clashed against the iron chest. Larsen went to it and picked it up. Rusty as it was, it would still cut after a fashion.

"Can you cook a chicken, Susie?"

"Try me and see."

"That's a bet. Chicken and yams! Sounds good. We'll use this to operate on the chicken. You haven't got a gun, by any chance?"

"Not likely. Haven't you?"

"Nope. Got nothing. All right, let's go. And after we eat, I'll get a hen fixed up properly and we'll start housekeeping this evening on your cooking. Say! No beds either. We'll have to fix up something. Do you want Gunn's rags to serve as blankets?"

She threw a glance at the ancient shape and shivered slightly.

"I do not."

"We're agreed on that point, anyhow. So long, Gimlet Eye! See you later."

There was no response; evidently the voice was not here.

UPON REGAINING the lower ground, Susan provided lunch from her own bundles, for her native edibles would not keep and rations would. Over the smoke that followed, she expressed her intention of having a swim in the lagoon.

"You go find a chicken and pluck and dress it, and stay up in the village," she said. Larsen cocked an eye at her.

"What if the ghost sees you?"

"Ghosts don't worry me. Other people do."

"All right. A shark may get you if you don't have anybody watching out to save your life. Or an octopus."

"I'll chance that." Her eyes twinkled. They were nice eyes, brown ones; her hair was brown, too, and braided about her head. "Is it a bargain?"

"All right," he said. "I'll be glad to see it happen, too."

"See what happen?"

"See Gimlet Eye come to life. He will, you bet. He has an eye for a wench, Susie."

Susan eyed him, a trace of red creeping up her cheeks.

"I'm not joking. And you'd better not, either. This is a serious matter."

"That's true enough. Old Gimlet Eye has been sitting up on that hill for two hundred years or so, and if he comes down to join you at your diversions you can bet it will be serious—"

Larsen grabbed the cutlass and took to his heels, just in time to evade a chunk of coral that whizzed past his ear. He made for the village and stayed there.

Being a Brooklyn lad by training, he had never in his life had any dealings with chickens on the hoof. These creatures were by no means wild, but evidently guessed his intentions, and stopped at nothing to balk him. At length he ran down an indignant hen and by virtue of falling on her and grabbing with both hands, captured her, or thought he had done so; but Malay chickens, regardless of sex, are fighters.

"Damn you, I'd like to wring your neck!" he grunted, but did not know how so he went after the old cutlass. Instead of cutting off her head, he cut off her body and it flopped at him, gunner or no gunner, he ran. After a while he came back to the corpse and plucked it cold, more or less. He vaguely remembered something about singeing a chicken but had no fire, so pursued his task to the bitter end, after which he got out his pocketknife and went to work on the innards, largely a matter of by guess and by gosh.

He was still at this, amid a mass of feathers and blood, when Susan came upon the scene and with a burst of laughter relieved him of the mess. She was flushed and rosy and said she had enjoyed a swell dip and there was no sign of Gimlet Eye.

"You probably scared him into modest blushes," said Larsen, and went off to dig some yams. There were some already dug, which saved trouble. They had begun to mould but he scraped off the green film and washed them in the creek, as good as ever. Then firewood. Then he retrieved all his buried belongings and took them up to his own house, and with no further demands on his time, went for a swim himself.

He did not swim long because he could not get the thought of his buried ship and shipmates down below out of his head. He was worried over that voice and the mention of Dierschow, too, he came back and dressed in the warm sun and cursed Gunner Gunn with hearty emphasis. The cackling snicker answered him.

"In my day a seafaring man could use stronger language than that, my lad," said the voice. Larsen looked around.

"You go to hell, will you?" he requested impolitely of the trees.

"I've been there already and don't like it. That's why I'm back here," responded the voice. "A good tall tankard of rum, that's what you need. King Kaiwas used to make stiff palm wine for me, and it was good. No palms on the island now. There was no chicken blood on that cutlass of mine, either, when I had it. Coming up from Makassar, last voyage, we ran into a Dutch barque and boarded her, and the blade ran red from point to hilt; and now you defile it with chicken blood!"

"Come out and show yourself, will you?" snapped Larsen. He heard a cackling in the brush, and went for it on the jump, regardless of thorns, only to see a pig go bouncing away, and to hear the cackling mirth of the unseen Mr. Gunn, whom he damned heartily.

Anyhow, the chicken and yams were first-rate that evening, one spitted over a fire and the others baked in the ashes. Susan certainly could cook.

CHAPTER FIVE

D URING THE three following days nothing untoward happened and Gunner Gunn remained silent.

The two castaways did not do so badly. They reposed on beds of giant ferns and long grass which Larsen gathered, and under the influence of Susan Mason he quite recovered his usual good spirits; with every day his admiration of her increased. She knew a hundred deft ways of doing things, native fashion, that made life more agreeable.

Larsen lugged loads of firewood up to the shelf where Mr. Gunn reposed and made ready a beacon, against the unlikely event of a ship or planes showing up. He got out his fishing tackle that had been placed in the rubber boat; he could see plenty of fish close to hand but for lack of any craft was unable to catch them, whereat he damned old Gimlet Eye afresh. A few hundred yards down the beach, at the north side, was a jumbled mass of coral lumps, and a bit of reef which was bared at low tide, but a visit showed nothing of interest there, and he confined his explorations to the west beach and the two hills. That on the north provided nothing of appeal except a large spring that fed the creek, and was too steep to climb easily, so he desisted.

On the third evening they finished the rations and bundled provisions, and Susan suggested that he butcher a pig.

"I don't like pork that much," said Larsen. "I'm not tired of yams, yet. And there are fish, if we could get 'em. Don't desert islanders always catch oysters and such?"

SHE SHOOK her head. "Not according to the natives. The shellfish aren't recommended except for would-be suicides. Are you one?"

"Not while you're on hand, anyhow."

"Well, you'd better chase up something to cook tomorrow," she rejoined tartily.

A laugh came out of the shadows. "You'll have plenty to cook. Your rubber boat will be back. But keep away from the point of rocks, understand?" When he said this, Gimlet Eye sounded serious. "Keep well away from them, or I'll take your boat and never give it back again."

"Won't you come and join us, Mr. Gunn?" spoke up Susan. "We'd love to have you."

"Aye, lass, there's many a wench has bade me welcome," replied the voice. "But thanks for the invitation. I'll bide where I am, since two's company. Just for your kind word, I'll make you a gift of what I stole from King Kaiwas."

Susan looked around, unavailingly. "That is very kind of you."

"Aye, you're a polite sort of wench, damn if you ain't!" said he. "Very well, I make you a present of my old pistol, but look out you don't try to fire it without drawing the load and using a fresh flint. The mate to it exploded and killed poor Bosum Jem, it did, on account of him being careless that way."

"Thank you, I'll remember it," said she.

"And when those damned Japs come around, you'll be glad of old Gimlet Eye, lass. He'll handle 'em! He can lay a gun better than any man alive."

WITH THIS, Mr. Gunn apparently departed to his own place, wherever that was. "In a cave, probably," said Larsen with a grunt of scorn. Ghosts and bats seemed to get on well together.

"This thing is getting on my nerves, Susie," he went gloomily. "Darned if I'll believe in ghosts and they that steal boats! But what's the answer, except just that?"

"I don't know, but I'm sure there'll be one," she replied. "And it'll probably turn out to be something very simple and logical; it always does. It's easy to imagine things, and they always prove to be matter of fact in the end. What worries me is what's become of Dr. Bowe. The natives said that he arrived here all right, then vanished one day."

"Everything about this place is cockeyed," he growled. "That is, all but you. If it wasn't for you, I'd have gone off my nut."

"I don't think so, Pete. You're pretty well balanced. Suppose we just wait and see what the morning brings forth. Maybe the boat will be returned, like his promise said would happen. And remember, a real voice doesn't come from nowhere. It comes from a real mouth."

"All right. Mr. Gunn is real. So what? We know he's roosting up on the peak, and does he come down here to talk to us?"

She shook her head. "Not likely. I've never yet seen corpses walking and talking."

"Is there anything more unlikely than the assumption that someone is playing a joke on us? That doesn't make sense."

"No. I'm not saying it makes sense—but I'm sure the explanation will. We'd better be thankful we're not worse off and let it go at that. If these nights were cold, we'd be suffering. Were you in my house today?"

"Me?" he demanded in surprise. "Of course not. Why?"

"Somebody was. My things were rummaged over; nothing missing, but not the way I left them. What do you make of that?"

"Gimlet Eye, damn him! Or else a pig got in and nosed around."

"Maybe. Well, I'm going to curl up in my ferns like a squirrel."

"Squirrels don't curl. Goodnight, and if Mr. Gunn drops in, holler!"

She was strictly okay, thought Larsen, looking after her with a warm glow of liking. Not many gals would take all this funny business the way she took it. Level headed, too; this showed in the way she had come over here to find Dr. Bowe after diagnosing her own trouble.

Larsen crawled into his own hut and burrowed down amid the ferns and slept.

Her voice awakened him to sunlight and breakfast—a spot of coffee each. There had been some powdered coffee in the supplies packed with the boat; it would not last them long, but it was a lifesaver. Larsen crawled out, went to the creek, doused his head, and joined her by the fire.

"WHY SO early and cheerful?" he demanded.

"Oh, I was curious! I went down to the beach. And, Pete! Your rubber boat is back. Just as he said it would be! At least, I think that's what's floating out a little way from shore. No hurry about it," she added, as Larsen moved to jump up. "The tide's nearly at flood and the boat won't get far."

"Why on earth do you suppose he took it?"

She broke into merry laughter. "Oh, he was probably floating around with your friend Dierschow, trying to get a gun off the wreck of your plane!" She checked her bantering tone at sight of his quick wince. "I'm sorry, Pete!" Leaning over, she patted his hand in swift remorse. "I didn't stop to think; forgive me."

Larsen's grin flashed out at her.

"Forget it, Susie. I'm tickled that you're feeling so good. I'll grab my coffee and beat it. You keep clear of the lagoon for a while, will you?"

She nodded, an impish look in her eyes. "Sure! You can have it all to yourself. I'm going over to the west beach and have a dip. But mind you don't go floating around and fishing without your clothes! I don't want a sunburned patient on my hands!

And if you get any fish, you clean them before you fetch 'em
home."

"Okay. I'll take that roast yam we had left over last night for
bait, till I get a piece of fish to use. So long!"

He departed in eager excitement and ran to the beach. Sure
enough, there it was, floating a hundred feet offshore!

With a shout of delight he stripped and took to the water. As he dashed in, he came to a halt, waist-deep, and then looked around. Here, washing in on the flood tide, were odds and ends of debris—bits of paper and splintered wood, and the brown waxed paper from a ration-container. Curious! They must have washed out of the wrecked plane, he thought, and pursued his way.

Five minutes later he was hauling himself into the rubber boat. In it lay one of the paddles, and the whole inside of the doughnut was dripping wet. And, rolling around loosely, he saw a .50 calibre machine-gun cartridge. He flopped in, and lay there warming in the sun and staring at this cartridge.

Where had it come from? Certainly it had not been there when he lost the boat. And who had been using the craft so recently that it was slopping wet? There was only one answer. He remembered, too, what the voice had said—"I'm going fishing for a gun from your ship one of these nights." Had Mr. Gunn really been doing this—did this explain the cartridge and the wet boat and the debris floating inshore?

"That guy will drive me nuts yet," said Larsen resignedly, and sat up, reaching for the paddle.

THE BOAT had drifted, probably with a current, up to the north end of the lagoon and close to the jumbled pile of coral rocks there. As Larsen sat up, he was facing these rocks—and had a momentary glimpse of something that paralyzed him. It was a face, looking square at him from those rocks; a face with wild staring eyes and long matted beard. Even as he sighted it, the thing was gone. It was there, then it was not there. He blinked, then his panic passed. A slow grin came to his lips, as he recalled the repeated injunction to keep away from those rocks.

"Okay, Gimlet Eye," he sang out. "I'll keep away, but if you do any more prowling around Susie's house you'll get your eyes blacked. Mind it!"

He had no response, and wanted none. A surge of relief and delight went through him as he fell to work. That face, those eyes, had supplied the missing answer. They had to deal with a harmless lunatic of some kind who was wandering about the island, probably living in caves, and fancied himself to be Mr. Gunn.

By the time he reached the shore, Larsen's exultation began to fade. The explanation did sound plausible and was probably correct more or less; but it did not fit all the facts, nor did it seem likely that another human could be inhabiting the island and still remain unseen and leave no traces.

"Oh, well, anything's possible with a screwball!" reflected Larsen, as he got into his clothes, or part of them. Thus dismissing the whole matter, very happily too, he put his fishing lines and baked yam into the boat and shoved out. Maybe Gimlet Eye had managed to get one of the guns out of the wreck; he seemed nuts about guns, and that cartridge would hint as much. What of it? He was clearly harmless.

Thereafter, for a space, Gunner Larsen of Brooklyn found everything rosy, and when he got the boat over toward the reef the fishing was so good that it astonished him. The first thing he caught was a little octopus as big as his hand; using bits of this for bait, he began to haul in real fish, to his immense delight.

Half an hour later he came ashore, carefully pulled up the boat above high water level, and scooped out a shimmering mess of fish. He stripped a length of vine and strung them on it, then started for camp. A voice—the voice—leaped out at him.

"Ho, shipmate! Ahoy there! You'd best clap on all sail and sharp about it, for the wench has need of you! Blow me and swivel me if she didn't get caught in a surf roll and get pounded on the bottom!"

Larsen made no response, but he hurried. At the village there was no sign of Susan; dropping the fish, he pushed on, calling to her. No answer came, nor did Gimlet Eye speak up again.

Coming to the west beach, Larsen saw that a high, heavy surf was rolling in, and sharp alarm tugged at him. The voice might have told the truth at that. He glanced along the shore and saw no sign of her, hurried on across the sand—then sighted something inert and white, half awash and drifting out with the now ebbing tide.

He damned old Gimlet Eye no more.

## CHAPTER SIX

GETTING THAT senseless figure to shore was no light task; luckily, she had not drifted out beyond the surf.

The big combers rolled in and broke with terrific bursting force. If she had been caught and pounded on the bottom, as might easily happen to a careless swimmer, there was explanation enough of her plight.

Larsen got her inshore at last, pulled her upon the sand. Her clothes were weighted down under a bit of rock, close by; she wore only a thin garment. Larsen heaped up sand, laid her over it face down, and went to work pressing and expanding her lungs. Her face was bruised, her arms and shoulders cut and scratched—Gimlet Eye had called the turn and no mistake.

After a moment she coughed up sea-water and sneezed lustily.

"God bless you!" said Larsen, and fetched her clothes, and spread them over her, then climbed into his own things. She had not come around, but her heart was beating and he knew she was all right. He knelt, looking down at her face; then suddenly leaned over and touched his lips to hers, and stood up.

"About my only chance, I guess," he observed. "Golly! What a sweet kid you are! You'd better wake up or I'll be tempted to do it over again."

Her arm moved; she flung a hand over her face, and struck the bruise above her eyes, and the pain evidently awakened her, for a groan escaped her and she opened her eyes. With a quick movement, she sat up, staring open-mouthed at Larsen.

"Oh! You—how—what happened?" she exclaimed.

"Don't ask questions. I don't know." Larsen got a cigarette alight and handed it to her. "Gimlet Eye said you needed help, and so you did. I pulled you up and emptied your lungs, and if you'll come along to camp I'll get some first aid dope on those bruises. He said a wave rolled you over."

"He said? Yes, it did. Then he must have been watching me!"

"Nope," said Larsen. "He was over by the lagoon. I saw him. Do you get that? I saw the guy! At least, a face looked out at me, all whiskers and big staring eyes. That settles the mystery. Mr. Gunn is just a loony who believes he's Gimlet Eye, probably made up the whole yarn, like some of these guys who think they're Napoleon."

Clutching her garments to her, Susan stared at him.

"So that's it! But how—"

"Never mind questions, Susie. Hop into your duds and come along."

"Oh! Do you think I'm going to dress in front of you?"

"Okay, behind me then." Larsen rolled over and turned his back. "You don't need to be so durned modest anyhow. Your bathing suit wasn't any overcoat. And I saved your life for you—"

A shower of sand hit him. "So it was you that kissed me! I thought it was a dream and—oh! I could wring your neck, Pete Larsen!"

Larsen made no response; he was clawing sand from the unwrung neck and smothering curses. Then, when she declared herself ready, he came erect to find her eyes twinkling at him and her cheeks dimpling.

"Thanks for saving my life—and everything," she said, breaking into a laugh. "Oh, Pete, I do like you a lot! But I'm all scratched up and bumped and sore—I thought sure I was done for when I was rolled around under that surf!"

Larsen grinned, and they were friends.

"Fish fry for lunch," he said. "Oh, boy! Will they taste good!"

"I hope so. Salt might improve them," she observed, as they started along the trail. "And this afternoon I'm going to go up the hill again."

"Want to sleep in a cave with the bats?"

"No, silly. I want to get the pistol Mr. Gunn gave me. I bet he had a reason for it. And he was the cause of saving my life wasn't he?"

Larsen grunted. "You'd better lay off being so durned polite to that guy. He's worse looking than old Whiskers up above. And—say, I'd bet he did break into the wreck of our plane, too!"

He told her about the cartridge and the floating stuff. Probably the lagoon was now very deep; at the same time, it did look like a crazy piece of business. They were still discussing this when they came to the village, and Larsen chased off a pig that was rooting around the fish, and went for his first aid kit.

"You lay bare your upper works and I'll fix up the cuts and bruises. Apparently the fuselage wasn't injured, but your wings sure need attention."

She complied, and he anointed the scratches and bruise on her forehead, while she laughed into his eyes and commented on his lack of skill. Then he went to work at the fish beside the creek. No pan fry unless he provided a skillet, and Susie, it was bake or nothing. So bake it was, and they both enjoyed the results exceedingly, and sat over a smoke together afterward. There was, naturally, only one topic of conversation.

"I had a notion from the start that there was a lunatic around, either me or him," said Larsen. "I'm glad it's him. As I figured, he found papers or something in that chest and pretty soon convinced himself that he was Weston Gunn. And yet—"

SUSIE NODDED as he paused, her eyes thoughtful.

"Yes. And yet! That theory just doesn't account for a lot of little things. How, for instance—"

"Don't ask questions!" barked Larsen. "I'm sick of asking myself questions that have no answer. I know it doesn't account for some things. But it makes others plausible. Only a lunatic would think of diving, apparently at night, to get a gun from the wreck; and those guns aren't easy to get, either. And how did he know you were in trouble, when he was here on this side of the island? And how does he know all that Gunner Gunn rigmarole which sounds so natural and truthful?"

"I thought you said not to ask questions?" Her eyes were dancing at him now. "I think we can prove up something by getting that pistol he gave me. Remember, he said he had put into it what he stole from King Somebody."

"King Kaiwas," said Larsen. "That was all hogwash."

"Maybe not. I'm going to see for myself."

"Do you want me to get the pistol for you?"

"No, we'll both go get it, after I lie down for an hour. Suit you?"

Larsen regarded her for a moment. "Susie, about anything you say or do suits me. That is how I feel about it. I'm nuts like Mr. Gunn, I think; I've known you for two or three hundred years, maybe longer."

Her eyes widened on him. "I hope you find me better preserved than he is?"

"Heaps!" Larsen chuckled, and came to his feet. "See you later. I'm going to try and find you that skillet. When you get ready to climb, I'll be at the beach."

He sauntered off, repressing an inclination to light another cigarette. Smokes were running low.

IN SHIRT and shorts he got into the boat and paddled out. As he had thought, the lagoon was not too deep, with the tide fast going out, to see the bottom. It was not long before he found what he was looking for—the wreckage of the bomber.

She had gone down hard enough to be ripped to pieces on the sharp coral; he could see little except wreckage. A diver would not have far to go in order to reach her. Yes, it was possible after all. He could see nothing of any guns, however.

He went on, out to where the reef that stopped the surf was exposed at low tide. Here he explored, with care; there were pools and pits in the coral, and after some search he came upon just the thing he was after—half a huge shell, glinting white and purple, that would make a good pot or skillet. He salvaged it and worked his way back to the beach. He would get some more fish later on, he figured; maybe take Susie out fishing.

"No you won't," said the voice of Gunner Gunn. Larsen peered around sharply and saw nothing at all.

"Won't what?" he demanded.

"Take the wench out fishing. Not unless you do it before sunset. Tomorrow you'll not have the chance."

"What the devil! Are you a mind-reader?" Larsen riposted.

The voice laughed. "Gimlet Eye Gunn knows all that's going on, shipmate."

"Listen, come off that Gunn stuff, will you?" Larsen was angry. "I got a glimpse of you, so you needn't hide out and think you can impress me. Come on into sight and talk like a white man."

"I am a white man, lad. My father was a wheelwright in Devon, and I'm as white as you, so don't be impudent. I warn you, take good care of that cutlass o' mine; you'll have better use for it than sticking hens, ere long."

"Yeah. Sticking pigs," said Larsen irreverently.

"No; better game than that, matey. And when those Japs show up, you lay low and leave 'em to Gunner Gunn, savvy?"

"What Japs?"

"The ones that are heading this way. Remember, leave 'em to me! I've waited two hunnerd year for this day and I don't want my fun spoiled."

"You're off the beam. Get wise to yourself," retorted Larsen. Mr. Gunn's laugh cackled and died away.

The boat pulled well up on the white sand in the center of the beach, Larsen took the big shell and headed for the village. He was irritated anew by thought of Mr. Gunn as a mind-reader; still, maybe he had thought out loud about taking Susie fishing, he reflected. Or the unseen speaker might have hit the mark with a long shot. This notion made him feel more cheerful about it all.

Japs? Nonsense. There were none here, and none were likely to come here. He very well knew that all the Japs in these waters were having a very tough time of it, thanks to Uncle Sam's fleets by sea and air. There was no reason for any Japs to come here, and nothing to come for.

He found Susie rested, and drying her hair in the sun, told her about it, and showed her the big shell. She agreed with him that any talk of Japs coming here was most likely just so much hot air.

"Still, anything's possible. And, Pete!" she went on. "I think I've hit the explanation of our friend Gunn."

"Tell me, and I'll tell you whether you have or not," said he.

"Not ready yet; let me think it out a little further. Do you know anything about psychology?"

"Just enough to know that you're the prettiest picture I ever saw, right now."

She smiled, and began to braid her hair. "Thanks for the skillet. If it doesn't go to pieces in the fire, it ought to work. So Mr. Gunn thinks we'd better go fishing this afternoon, does he? Not a bad idea. I'd enjoy it—after we get the pistol."

"Okay," said Larsen. "Mind if I ask a personal question?"

"That depends. Ask it and see, Pete."

"Well," he hesitated awkwardly. "It's like this. How free are you?"

"Free?" She eyed him questioningly. "I was born free, Pete."

"Sure. That wouldn't prevent me, for example, being tied up to a gal, only I'm not. I did have one in Brooklyn but she married a Marine. What about you?"

"Oh, is that what you mean!" She broke into laughter, and went on with her hair. "Well, Pete, this is a desert island except for Mr. Gunn, and if we're not rescued for five or ten years I expect we'll have to get married, just to be conventional—won't we?"

"Hell's bells, I didn't ask you to joke about it," he observed stiffly.

"You certainly didn't expect me to be serious about it, did you?" she rejoined in severe accents. "At least here in broad daylight." Her eyes twinkled. "You ought to reserve such questions for moonlight or at least starlight, with the romantic whisper of waves on the beach— Oh, Pete! Help—there's an ant between my toes and it's biting—"

Larsen stooped to the rescue and they both broke into a gale of laughter. But a red ant stuffed with explosive formic acid is no joke; Susie was limping for the rest of the afternoon.

## CHAPTER SEVEN

ONCE MORE they climbed the winding trail that led up the south peak.

Larsen regarded this business of the pistol as pure nonsense, and said so, but Susie was stubborn about it. Anyhow, said she, the pistol would make a grand memento to keep, and she meant to have it and whatever was in it.

"Are you going nuts too?" Larsen asked rudely, as he climbed along behind her. "If there is a powder charge and a bullet, it'll be spoiled long ago."

"Oh, you don't understand at all, Pete! I've formed a theory, and I think it may be correct. If Gunn really stole something from King Kaiwas and stuffed it into that big pistol—"

"Rats!" cut in Larsen impatiently. "This maniac running around loose wouldn't know anything about it. He's just trying a hoax."

"I don't think so. Why not wait and see, before we argue? Anyhow, it'll prove my theory either right or wrong."

"Okay," he said, and let it go at that.

It was early afternoon, brilliant sunlight was beating down on the island, and the widespread sea below was a rich, surf-tipped blue; not at all the sort of day in which to indulge rattlebrained fancies. Larsen kept an eye on the holes in the rock. He was getting fed up with the place, and for lack of other occupation was thinking about trying a bit of exploration. Those caves might be interesting.

"If our tame lunatic found old Gimlet Eye in one of them, no telling what we might find," he said.

"He's not a lunatic," she rejoined firmly. "However, we won't argue it now. Isn't it lovely up here, after the dead heat down in the valley? This sea breeze is grand! I'd like to live up here all the time!"

"With the bats?" queried Larsen. "You need an elevator with a penthouse, Susie."

"Why must you be so dreadfully practical? Aren't you even a little bit romantic?"

Larsen grunted. "Too much so, maybe. Five or ten years from now I might let myself go and be all romantic."

He heard her bubbling laugh but she made no reply.

THEY REACHED the shelf at last, where Mr. Gunn sat keeping his eternal lookout to the southern skies. Larsen, who had fetched along some bits of wood, added these to the pile at one side to serve as beacon if the chance came to make a signal, then joined her in front of the blank-faced figure with its staring blue eyes of vigil.

"It seems almost too bad to leave him without any weapon at all," said Susie. "Look, this pistol is wired to his hand—"

The thin wire was weak with rust. It was easily broken loose from the leathery old paw of Mr. Gunn, and Susie took the long-barreled pistol. This was very green with corrosion, but the bore was enormous in size.

"Brass," commented Larsen. "Boy! Look at the size of the bore! Darned near fifty calibre, I'll bet. One of those bullets would sure blow daylight into a guy. What's that black patch in the handle?"

Susie rubbed the black smear set into the butt, and a glitter rewarded her.

"It's a silver plate, Pete! Give me a rag or something—"

"Use your skirt. It's your gun, not mine."

With a grimace, she complied, rubbing away at the silver until it came partly clear and revealed a name neatly chased. "Weston Gunn, 1744" it read. Larsen looked at it and nodded.

"The guy was real, all right. Is there any load inside?"

The flintlock hammer would not work. Sticking his finger down the bore, Larsen felt stoppage, and got out his pocket-knife. This had a corkscrew blade which was long enough to reach the stoppage. He worked away and presently drew out the knife and some bits of rotten cloth.

"Something there, sure enough, Susie! The knife won't reach any farther. Here, I'll get a stick."

His pile of wood yielded a thin stick, and they worked away, getting nothing except more of the ancient cloth. Susie's eyes were dancing excitedly; she took the stick and went at the job with determination, while Larsen went down the trail until he could see the western horizon. The ocean was all blank and empty, the loom of land westward was more distinct than usual; he could make out mountains against the horizon. A sudden cry from Susie reached him.

"Pete! Come here, quick!"

He hurried back. More cloth, and some tufts of cotton, lay in her lap; she was staring at something in her palm, and held it out to him.

"Look! Look at these—they rolled out—they were stuffed in with the cotton—diamonds, Pete! And two pearls!"

She could scarcely speak for excitement, and no wonder. Larsen looked down at two shimmering, iridescent globules as large as peas, and half a dozen stones of larger size that flashed dully in the sunlight.

"Diamonds?" he repeated. "By gosh! Say, they don't look like much to me. I've seen better looking diamonds from a dime store. But those two pearls are beauties."

"They're all beauties!" she exclaimed. "The diamonds are the old rose cut, or table, cut stones, like all very old ones. They're not very valuable, compared to diamonds as they're cut today, but they're real, and they're lovely."

It was some time before her ecstasy could calm down, as they discussed the stones one by one and fingered them in the sunlight. Then she looked up at him, her lips half-parted, her cheeks flushed.

"Pete, I guess this does prove my theory."

"You win, sister," he said. "Whatever the theory is, you win."

"It's split personality," she rejoined. "This poor fellow whom you call a lunatic is someone who perhaps got badly hurt. Maybe his head was injured. His own personality dropped out of sight, and the personality of Gunn took hold of him. To all intents and purposes he *is* Gunn. That would explain everything, even how he knew what was here in the pistol. Do you see?"

Larsen stared at her. "Is that stuff scientific?"

"Well, it is in a way. A split personality is recognized—"

"Personality be hanged," said Larsen. "I don't savvy your line. It's just the same as I've said all along—the guy is a lunatic."

"But it's not the same!" she protested. "He's no lunatic. For the time being, he actually is Weston Gunn, Pete. He'll come out of it—maybe with some sudden shock, maybe with an operation—"

"All right; now you listen to me a minute," he broke in, smiling. "You stick to your theory, I'll stick to mine. Let's leave it like that. Doesn't matter a durn who's right and who's wrong, but it matters a lot if we get worked up and lose our tempers. I don't want to get into a row with you for another couple hundred years, maybe longer. Suit you?"

Her features rippled with mirth. "Don't you think I could hold my own in a row?"

"Sure. But you're so sweet and nice, Susie, that I don't ever want to row with you," he said gravely.

She gave him a quick look. "Why, I believe you mean it! Thanks, Pete. I don't know about being sweet, but I think you're nice. It's a bargain. Now, what'll I do with these things?" She held up the gems in her palm.

"I'd say put 'em back where they come from. You can always hang on to the pistol and nobody will think twice about it."

"Good head!" She fell to work, wrapping diamonds and pearls in the bits of ancient cotton again and carefully stuffing them down the pistol-barrel, then sending the pieces of rotten cloth after them. "There! No danger of losing them now. Shall we go? I'm looking forward to that fishing trip, Pete."

"So'm I," he said. "Come along."

THEY STARTED down the trail together. From the shelf where Mr. Gunn stood watch, the eastern beach and lagoon, and the farther sea in that direction, was invisible; but a little below, as the descending path turned the side of the peak, it all came into sight. Larsen halted.

'By golly, I'll have to hand it to the guy! He said Japs were coming—and there they are!"

He pointed to a smoke that broke the far northeast horizon. Then, as Susie said nothing, he turned to her. To his astonishment she was white as death; her eyes were dilated upon the smoke, and she was quivering from head to foot.

"Good lord! What's wrong with you, Susie?" he demanded. She took a deep breath.

"Japs—you scared me, Pete, Japs!" she said unsteadily. "I thought you really saw them coming. You don't know what it does to one—after being a prisoner—after being in a concentration camp so long—I guess my heart just turned over."

"Why, you poor kid!" Swift compassion seized him; he reached out and patted her arm, awkwardly. "I just said that, about Japs. Maybe that smoke isn't coming this way at all. They're not likely to be Japs, anyhow. We cleaned all those lice off the ocean up Leyte way and sent 'em crawling home. Cheer up and forget it. I didn't know how you felt."

She forced a smile. "Sorry, Pete. I just can't help it, I guess. I thought I could take anything, but well, I just can't stand the thought of Japs again, and it knocked me cold for a minute. I'm all right now."

"Sure you are. Come along, and forget all about that smoke. It doesn't mean anything—probably one of our ships going by. If it comes any closer, I'll send up a smoke from the beacon."

She clutched at his arm. "No, no, don't do that! It might—might be a Jap ship and might draw them."

"Okay," said Larsen without demur, and started on down the trail. He did not blame her a mite for being upset. By the stories he had heard from occupants of Jap concentration and prison camps, they were plain hell; it was a wonder she could be as bright as she normally showed herself.

They came clown to the beach, got hooks and bait, shed their footgear and started out in the rubber dinghy. From here, the horizon smoke was not visible at all.

Larsen paddled nearly out to the reef, then drifted, and when Susie pulled in the first fish, her delight was something to see. Her foot was still swollen from the ant bite and Larsen inspected it.

"Most people's feet are ugly as the devil. Yours are pretty," said he critically. "Good to look at. Same as your face."

"So I have a face like a foot, have I?" she retorted.

Larsen chuckled.

"You should worry, gal. There goes your line—pull on it!"

The fish bit ravenously. An hour passed, and they had more than enough for their wants. Susie suggested keeping at it and leaving some on the beach for Gimlet Eye, so they tarried longer and hauled in more fish, until Larsen, who had quietly been keeping an eye on the eastern horizon, saw what he feared.

"You paddle back, while I get some of these fish cleaned," he said, and she complied laughingly, and made a good job of it. This, naturally, kept her facing toward the shore.

When they reached it, Larsen maneuvered with no little skill to give her no chance of looking seaward, and finally thrust upon her the fish he had already cleaned.

"Take these along, and I'll follow with the rest," he said. "You can be looking up some small firewood, and I'll get more when I come along."

"Right," she said, and departed.

When she was out of sight, Larsen drew a breath of relief and stood up, looking seaward. No doubt about it; the smoke was a smudge, and was coming closer.

"I told you them Japs would be along," said the voice of Mr. Gunn, from nowhere.

CHAPTER EIGHT

"**A**REN'T YOU man enough to come out and show yourself?" demanded Larsen.

"Not me, shipmate. You can see all o' me you want up on the hill," replied Mr. Gunn with a cackle. "You keep that old cutlass of mine handy, mind, and if a pinch comes, you can take to the caves wi' the lass. A proper wench she is! But don't let the Japs scare you, and don't bother with 'em. Gimlet Eye Gunn will take care of them."

"You're a bit previous. We don't know that this smoke means Japs. Maybe it's one of our own craft."

"You'll see, matey. A half disabled Jap ship full o' guns, that's what she is, running from the fight. Trust to Gunner Gunn and keep your chin up. There'll be no fight till morning. See you later."

"Loony as they come," reflected Larsen, irritated as usual by the voice. "It's a wonder he didn't tell the color of the Japs' eyes and hair! All bosh. Most likely it's one of our own sub-chasers or P.T. boats. Still, we don't want to get Susie worked up about it; a darned lucky thing she wasn't here to overhear that loony talk. I hope the guy has cleared out for good. Still, one thing he said did make sense—about the caves."

He left some of the fish; he had forgotten to tell Mr. Gunn about them, but that did not matter. With the rest, he made for the village and found Susie hard at work. He gave his personal attention to the fire, without ostentation, carefully selecting only dry wood that would make little smoke, and hoped for the best.

The big shell served its purpose admirably. Susie, flushed and adorable, turned out a perfectly scrumptious fish dinner that made even the iron-hard ration biscuits taste like something. The cooking done, Larsen thoughtfully doused the fire.

"You're a swell cook, Susie," he said. "I'm going to be real sorry when we get rescued."

"The larder isn't very extensive," she said. "You'd better make up your mind to butcher a pig. The cutlass would do."

"Maybe we can get Gimlet Eye to do it for us. How you feeling?"

"Tight like a drum," she said, laughing. "Why?"

"Just wondered." He looked up, and suppressed a groan. The stars were out, night had come, but he caught a radiance that touched the peaks above and was gone. "Y'know, Susie, there might be some bad news for you."

"Meaning what, Pete? Oh, look! Is that moonlight already? On the high trees?"

"Nope. Moon is about full and won't be up till later," he said, and sighed. "Darn it all! I was hoping it wouldn't come true, but I guess that settles the matter. I had a chat with Gimlet Eye after you left me, or he had a chat with me. He was quite positive that the Japs were on the way. A disabled destroyer or some such craft, he said."

"Oh, I see." She was silent for an instant. "All right, Pete. Let's have it. You mean the light that comes and goes?"

"I'm afraid so. They may be running to find shelter inside the reef, and using the searchlight. If there's an opening in the reef, they'd know it. Those ringtails know everything about all these islands."

"Well," she said after a minute, "I guess we'd better know the worst, hadn't we? Shall we go over to the beach and see?"

"That's the girl. You don't need to go. You can stay here. Scared?"

"Horribly," she admitted. "But I'd sooner go with you."

"All right. Fine! Give me your hand and I'll pilot you."

He took her hand, and it was cold. He knew she was hard hit.

"You knew all the time that smoke was coming, didn't you?" she asked.

"Saw it while we were fishing."

They said no more, but followed the path to the beach. And, when they emerged into the open, the worst was fairly obvious. They stood looking, still hand in hand.

The ship had come close; it showed no lights, but the radiant finger of a searchlight was touching the water, a little to the southward; evidently the reef-channel had been picked up and the vessel was coming in for shelter.

"Let's not holler till we're hurt," Larsen said quietly. "We're taking a lot for granted; may be one of our own ships putting in to make repairs. Let's sit down, and be comfortable, till we learn the truth. They won't attempt a landing tonight, anyhow. If they do, we can take to the caves, remember."

They stretched out in the warm sand, watching that finger of light. Then, under the stars, they could see the black blob of the ship itself; it was coming slowly through the reef opening. The searchlight swept up, touched on the peaks and the beach, and Larsen was glad of the leafy screen that sheltered them from watching binoculars.

The thrum of engines fell quiet. The rattle of chain going out, the heavy splash of an anchor, reached them; the searchlight was abruptly doused. Voices came across the water to them—the chattering voices of Japanese. Pete Larsen heard his companion gasp, then her hand came searching for him.

"Japs, sure enough! Pete, I—I'm frightfully scared—I can't stand it, Pete! I can't stand it—"

Her arms came around him, her head was against his chest; she was sobbing in dry gasps. He held her to him, saying little, trying to hearten her. He patted her cheek and found it wet, and kissed it.

"I'll see you safe, sweetheart," he said, with a tenderness he had never suspected in himself. "We'll see it through together. Just don't you think about them at all; shut your eyes and think about Des Moines and everything you're going back to, one of these fine days."

So he talked soothingly, as to a child, while she clung to him and her gasping breath quieted. After a long while he realized that she must be asleep; and very carefully, in order not to disturb her, he stretched out and made himself comfortable in the sand.

There were no sounds of any disembarking from the vessel. A faint sound of metal and hammering came from her; they must be at work on her engines, he reflected, losing no time in getting at repairs. Perhaps they would not come ashore at all, and upon this comforting thought he dozed off.

HE AWAKENED with a start, to the chill breath of dawn. The skies were gray. Susie lay with her arms still around him, and she was smiling as she slept. For a little, Larsen did not move. He did not want to wake her, but knew that he must. He bent his head and kissed her, felt her arms tighten about him and her eyes opened. She looked up at him and smiled, then alarm flashed into her face.

"It's all right, Susie," he said. "Morning now. Sorry I had to wake you."

"Good heavens! Have I been asleep here—"

He kissed her again. She responded, and smiled anew into his eyes.

"Thank you, Pete. You're a dear boy. I was terribly panicky, wasn't I? Now I think I'll be all right."

He helped her to rise. They looked at the vessel lying so close.

"You run along," he said. "There's still a little coffee powder left; make a tiny fire. I'll stay and keep an eye on things, and be along after a while."

"All right," she replied, and departed.

Larsen retreated out of sight of the vessel, and got the stiff-ness out of his bones with a few setting-up exercises, then came back to a point of vantage. The vessel was a destroyer, long and slim and battle-gray. She was low in the water, and most of her amidships section and bridge was a tangled mass of gaunt wreckage.

"Oh, boy! She got a bomb, all right; too bad it wasn't a bigger one," he thought. "Disabled her but didn't cripple her engines."

Whistles sounded and she came to life; the sun was just showing in a rim of golden scarlet.

Men moved about her decks. The off-sea breeze stirred the sunrise flag at her stern and brought to Larsen's nostrils the odors of food cooking. This reminded him, and he made his way back to the village, pausing en route for a hasty wash at the creek. He found a tiny fire ablaze, water bubbling over it in the big shell, and Susie greeted him brightly.

"Good morning! All ready? This will finish up the coffee. What news?"

"Nothing very bad," he replied. "Looks like a destroyer that caught a bomb and she needs repairs. We won't need to worry for a while, anyhow."

"Think they'll come ashore?"

He nodded. "Sure. For fresh water if for nothing else."

She mixed the coffee and they took turns drinking from the shell. Larsen got out the cigarettes, and these were down to three. He cut one in two.

"Might as well finish 'em. Can't smoke if we're hiding out."

She nodded, held a brand for a light, then scattered the fire, scooping sand upon it. They sat smoking.

"So this is the end of our desert island peace!" she observed. "I'd give a good deal if I had a gun, Pete. I could use it."

He started. "Hello! I forgot about Gimlet Eye. Wonder if he really did get a gun out of our ship? He said to trust him, that he'd take care of the Japs. That guy is liable to go nuts and get us all blown to hell. Have you got some matches?"

"Yes. Why?"

"You may have to take charge of the beacon near Mr. Gunn, up above. That spot isn't visible from where the destroyer lies. If they do come ashore, I want you to get up there and take to the caves—"

"I'll not!" she flashed out.

"Yes you will, too. There may be one of our ships or planes coming along to look up this Jap baby and we'll have to light the beacon. I'll depend on you."

She gave up protest. "All right, then. But we'll keep an eye on them first."

They finished their smoke. He stood up. "Ready?"

"No. Anything but. No help for it, though."

She threw him a quick smile. "All set, Pete! Got your cutlass? Let's go."

## CHAPTER NINE

T HEY CAME into sight of the beach and lagoon. Larsen led the way carefully to a spot under cover of the brush. Dropping into the sand, they wormed forward and got a complete view of the destroyer.

Larsen made an effort to count the Japs who were swarming over her wreckage. Mighty close to a hundred, he figured; she must have lost plenty. They were hard at work getting wreckage cleared away. Some of her guns were disabled. It was not hard to guess that she was here making only temporary repairs, perhaps to her controls, in order to make a run for Singapore or elsewhere and get a thorough working over.

The vessel was lying a little south of the beach, not more than a hundred yards offshore. The voices of the Japs reached clearly across the water. An officer amid the bridge wreckage shouted an order, and Susie gasped.

"Pete! He said to make the boats ready. They're coming ashore!"

"How d'you know what he said?"

She shivered. "You spend three endless years in a prison camp, and you'll speak Japanese too. Had we better make for the caves?"

"Not yet," he replied. "Take it easy. I'm curious to see if old Gimlet Eye will do anything. So far he's called the turn every time. Maybe he will again."

They lay waiting and watching; it was nervous work.

The activity aboard the vessel paused. Voices called back and forth; Susie translated. Only two boats were serviceable, the others were destroyed. First one, then another boat was put out, with some difficulty, having to be lowered by hand. Men swarmed into them, arms glittered, orders were given. Casks were sent down.

"Pete! They mean to stay!" muttered Susie, ashen-faced. "They're coming for water, also to occupy the island—"

"Okay," said Larsen. "Sit tight."

His composure heartened her. The two boats put forth oars and headed for the beach at the creek mouth, directly in front of where the two were hidden. As they came nearer, Larsen began to think about discretion. Might be best to sneak away and make for the peak. If he only had a rifle, he could hold that twisting trail against an army! But he had none. And if—

*Bam-bam-bam!*

Larsen jumped a foot, as a sharp, abrupt burst sounded. Fifty calibre, he thought. Around the boats, the water spurted. Wild yells went up—then the roaring staccato burst went on, filling the air with tumultuous sound. The machine-gun raked the two boats; the heavy bullets smashed flesh and wood alike. One boat sank. The other, filled with dead and dying men, drifted slowly toward shore. A few heads showed in the water, the remorseless gun battered them down. The drifting boat foundered in the shallows; nothing alive was left in her.

The destroyer broke into life. A machine-gun chattered; a Bofors gun was depressed and sent its needle shells roaring at the shore. Larsen, tensed, had seen where that deadly fire came from; the Japs saw too—from the jumbled pile of coral rocks at the north end of the lagoon. Shells burst, rock flew; the .50-calibre gun was silent.

Peace descended on the islet, after the blether of sound. The rank odor of cordite drifted across the lagoon. Already the Japs were in motion. A stream of them was taking to the water to swim ashore. Larsen reached out and touched the girl beside him.

"Get going," he said. "They've silenced him. Move! I'll be along."

She inched back, rose, and then disappeared.

Swimming, holding weapons above the water, the file of Japs was halfway to shore when, without warning, the pile of coral rocks again erupted fire and fury. Larsen marveled at how that bucking, jumping gun could be so perfectly controlled. Bullets swept the string of heads.

Instantly the destroyer's guns leaped into action, pouring a stream of fire at the unseen machine-gun. Its attention was switched to them. Its bullets raked their decks, struck down the gun crews, sowed death and destruction—then it fell silent. More shells burst all around it, but it gave back no reply.

"They got him," thought Larsen. Most of the swimmers had vanished. Then, rising, stooping low, he dashed forward across the beach.

The foundered boat was rolling over, spilling dead men and guns at the water's edge, and the temptation was too strong to be resisted. Larsen flung himself forward as he came to the water. He saw a rapid-fire carbine, with an attached drum, and grabbed it, rolled over, came up and took to his heels. As he reached the brush, machine-gun fire swept through the trees— they had seen him, all right.

He fell flat, worked his way ahead into the brush, and ran. Then he remembered that up above, one turn of the trail would involve full exposure to those below. He thought of Susie, and with leaping heart flung himself forward. That white dress of hers against the rock—

HE POUNDED up the trail as fast as he could leg it. Sure enough! The rattle of a machine-gun echoed from the lagoon; he heard the bullets whistle overhead. There was the open stretch—and she was across! The gun fell silent. Without a pause, Larsen went at it full tilt, put on his best spurt of speed—

and was halfway to safety when the gun began again. A second gun joined in. At the last dozen feet he lost his nerve and fell to his face, and crawled. Bullets were whining just above him—he could feel the wind of them, could hear the splashing crackle of them against the rock face.

But he came through safely, and then halted, regardless of Susie calling him forward.

The gun in his hands was strange to him, but he quickly got the hang of it. Then, face down, he inched forward to get sight of the lagoon. It came into his vision. He saw the destroyer lying almost under him, and sighted carefully at the group of men about the stern machine-guns. Then he let them have it—a quick burst, and another. He saw them falling, and stayed his hand, and hurriedly withdrew.

A deadly but totally ineffective fire was opened. Shells and bullets stormed against the cliff, searching out every foot of the exposed portion. Grinning delightedly, Larsen hopped ahead to where Susie was waiting.

"So you must have your fun, eh?" she said tartly. "Why did you have to risk your neck getting that gun, and then shooting it?"

"That's what it's for," he retorted. "And I needed it so no Japs could get along this path. Listen to the ringtails wasting shells on the rock!"

Then he stopped and suddenly was dragging her to the very verge of the trail, his eyes wild, his features contorted with excitement.

"Look!" he cried. "Look! Do you see what I do?"

He pointed to a triangle of dots against the southern sky. She looked at them.

"Yes, sure—you mean—"

"Get up there quick and light that beacon smoke! Quick!" he barked.

WITH NO further questions, she turned and ran. Larsen feasted his eyes on that triangle of planes. It seemed to him that they were swinging around as though to point this way— then he hurriedly went streaking back to where he could get a sight of the lagoon. The hail of bullets and shells had ceased. But, when he cautiously took a squint at the destroyer, he perceived why the planes might have turned, conceivably. Gimlet Eye Gunn must have had some explosive bullets; a plume of smoke was going up from the wreckage in her waist and the Japs were fighting it frantically. The gun crews had abandoned their guns to join in the work.

Larsen thought rapidly. No ghost had been working that .50-calibre gun, but it had remained silent. Now, with the Japs busy as the devil, was his chance to get down to the beach with his weapon and get around to that clump of rocks—

With an effort, he resisted. No. Gunner Gunn must take his chance; the Japs had seen him and Susie going up the trail and would have concentrated on the peak. If any of them had reached the shore, he must wait here. He dared not risk abandoning Susie to peril. He drew back, sighed, inspected his automatic rifle, and looked up again at the sky. He could not repress a yell of wild delight. They were coming, sure enough! And from the shelf, spiraling up above the peak, was ascending the signal-smoke—Susie had worked fast!

"Coming like bats out of hell—Lightnings!" he cried, distinguishing them now. "Oh, boy! If those Japs will only get rattled and go to shooting, there won't be any mistake about it—"

He waited, tense and agonized.

The triangle in the sky was certainly making for the island. The smoke had drawn their attention. Perhaps they were a patrol looking for remnants of the broken Jap fleet. The signal was mounting in black puffs, they could not miss it! Larsen stole forward once more, hoping desperately that the Japs would see their peril and open fire. He caught sight of the lagoon and the destroyer, and broke into frantic whispers of jubilation. The Japs had scattered to the guns.

The long muzzles of the Bofors guns were swinging and elevating; next moment they began to jump, and Larsen hugged himself.

Flak blossomed blackly in the sky. The twin-boomed Lightnings could make no error now, nor did they. Down they came and down, contemptuous of the bursts around them; then, no higher than the peaks of the island, they leveled off, and Larsen saw the tiny black dots of falling bombs, as the skies roared and the three ships angled sharply out of the flak and wheeled southward.

HE PUT down his weapon and danced excitedly, waving and yelling till he was hoarse.

The water spurted around the destroyer; then she vomited flame and smoke. The three Lightnings had already turned, and came back, swooping low. Their guns chattered into the belching smoke and they were gone.

Larsen turned and legged it up the trail in blazing excitement. He met Susie coming toward him, and seizing her, hugged her with jubilant, incoherent cries. They were at the turn, just below where Mr. Gunn sat, and a sudden roaring swept down at them as a Lightning swooped close. They waved frantically; the pilot dipped his wings in signal, and then zoomed away to rejoin his fellows.

"They're gone!" cried Susie in sudden dismay. "Pete—they're going! Leaving us!"

"Going? Sure. No place to stop here. But you can be sure they're talking now by radio, and we'll see either a Catalina or a P.T. come over the horizon before very long—come on, come on, look at the destroyer! She's done for!"

And he dragged her, laughing and talking at once, down the trail. They both quite forgot, in their excitement, that at least one or two of those Japs had come ashore.

## CHAPTER TEN

**S**MALL BLAME to them for the forgetting, either.
Just before they gained sight of the lagoon, a tremendous
bursting explosion sent flame high in air, scorching them,
rocking the very earth under them, and the concussion knocked
them both flat on the trail. A volume of black smoke belched
up; bits of wood, metal, flesh, came showering down on everything.

"She's gone up!" yelled Larsen hoarsely. "Hurray! Look, look!"

A little farther, and the lagoon opened before them; they
stood in stricken silence, staring at the incredible scene. The
destroyer was gone, indeed, and it was quite apparent that none
of the Japs who had been aboard her would reach shore. A pall
of oily smoke hung over the water; all of it was aflame. The
escaped oil and gasoline was burning fiercely there, sealing the
fate of any who had escaped the explosion.

"Lord!" exclaimed Larsen, delighted yet appalled. "That's the
way some of our ships went at Pearl Harbor."

"I lost a brother there," said Susie, very soberly.

"Well, you don't need to be scared of any Japs now. Look
here, let's go see what's happened to old Gimlet Eye! After all,
we owe him just about everything—maybe he's dead or
wounded. Must be, since he quit firing long ago."

"Yes, we owe him plenty," she assented, and stepped out.
Larsen, hugging the automatic rifle, followed closely.

The abrupt, deadening silence that hung over everything was significant. The offset breeze drifted the oily smoke from the lagoon across the beach and trees, and with it odors that made Susie wrinkle up her nose in acute distaste—odors of cordite and oil and burning flesh.

"Hey, where's your big pistol?" demanded Larsen suddenly.

She flung him a laughing glance over her shoulder. "Under the cooking shell, down at camp. I left it there on purpose."

"Okay. Look out for that piece of a Jap in the path ahead—"

Not a piece of a Jap, but a twisted fragment of metal, fallen from the debris of the explosion. She stepped around it and went on. The drift of burning oil darkened the sunlight and dimmed it overhead; the trees below looked almost foggy.

They came down without incident. Now, abruptly, Larsen remembered what he had feared about one or two Japs coming ashore from the swimming party. He said nothing but kept his finger on the trigger and probed the trees and brush with quick vigilance.

He began to regret his haste to look up Mr. Gunn. This oily mist along the beach was highly unpleasant. However, as they skirted the shore around to the clump of rocks and he discerned no sign of life anywhere, his alarm decreased. A lucky thing Gunn had blown their boats out of the water at the first go!

THEY REACHED the rocks, and here was clearer air, away from the oily murk. Clambering up, they came to the slightly higher level of the coral chunks—and there before them was dispelled the final mystery of Weston Gunn.

The machine-gun must have been struck squarely—it lay toppled over to one side. And near it, a smear of blood on his face, lay the dark, ragged figure whose face Larsen had glimpsed—a figure all tatters, barefoot, gaunt. Susie dropped on her knees beside it and a sharp cry escaped her.

"Pete! He's not dead—get some water, quick!"

Larsen clambered over the coral lumps and brought a cloth back dripping. He found Susie parting the long beard and carefully examining the sunken features. She took the wet cloth, began to mop the man's head, and gave Larsen an amazed glance.

"Look! It can't be—but it is!"

"Yeah. What?"

"Why, Doctor Bowe, of course! There's no shell wound, either. His head must have been struck by a piece of flying coral—it's a jagged hurt, but doesn't look like a concussion. Yes, it's Doctor Bowe—and he was right with us all the time—oh! There's a bad scar, near the new wound—"

She washed the hurt well and bound it up with the wet cloth. Then she turned and looked at Larsen, her eyes wondering.

"Do you see? It's exactly like I said. He hurt his head somehow, perhaps in getting Gunn's mummy out and put together—and that did it!"

"Knocked him insane, you mean?"

She frowned. "Well, if you want to put it that way, I suppose so. When he came to himself, he wasn't himself at all, but Gunn. Don't you see?"

Larsen nodded. "Sure. He was a lunatic, like I said."

"Oh, you're hopeless!" she said in an awed tone. "Gunn's personality had possession of him. I've heard of such things…."

She broke off sharply. A low groan came from the unconscious man. His eyes opened. He put a hand to his head, groaned again, then responded as Susie helped him to sit up. He stared blankly around.

"Hello! Where am I? What's happened?" he said. It was certainly not the voice of Mr. Gunn.

His eyes widened at sight of Susie. "Oh! It's Susan Mason— am I dreaming?"

Her bubbling laugh sounded. "No, Dr. Bowe, you're not dreaming. I'm here. Your head is hurt, you know."

"Yes, yes. I remember now," he said. "I was getting that skeleton or mummy down from the cave—must have been a nasty fall, but I don't remember—hello! Who's this man?"

LARSEN MET the stare with a grin.

"Why, you remember me, don't you? Aren't you Gimlet Eye Gunn?"

The other frowned. "Gunn? I never heard the name. No, I'm Clyde Bowe—"

He broke off, evidently bewildered and puzzled. Susan caught Larsen's eye and made violent signs not to say any more. He nodded in agreement. A miracle had happened, and explanations could come later. Rescue would also come in due course, but one thing he knew; between this girl and him there would always be a powerful bond; they would remember the secret, sacred island where the past merged with the present, hear again the voice of a long-dead gunner and his hoarse laughter echoing among the barren rocks. The war in the Pacific would mean for them the miracle of Gimlet Eye Gunn.

# ABOUT THE AUTHOR

**H**. BEDFORD-JONES is a Canadian by birth, but not by profession, having removed to the United States at the age of one year. For over twenty years he has been more or less profitably engaged in writing and traveling. As he has seldom resided in one place longer than a year or so and is a person of retiring habits, he is somewhat a man of mystery; more than once he has suffered from unscrupulous gentlemen who impersonated him—one of whom murdered a wife and was subsequently shot by the police, luckily after losing his alias.

The real Bedford-Jones is an elderly man, whose gray hair and precise attire give him rather the appearance of a retired foreign diplomat. His hobby is stamp collecting, and his collection of Japan is said to be one of the finest in existence. At present writing he is en route to Morocco, and when this appears in print he will probably be somewhere on the Mojave Desert in company with Erle Stanley Gardner.

Questioned as to the main facts in his life, he declared there was only one main fact, but it was not for publication; that his life had been uneventful except for numerous financial losses, and that his only adventures lay in evading adventurers. In his younger years he was something of an athlete, but the encroachments of age preclude any active pursuits except that of motoring. He is usually to be found poring over his stamps, working at his typewriter, or laboring in his California rose garden, which is one of the sights of Cathedral Cañon, near Palm Springs.

www.ingramcontent.com/pod-product-compliance
Lightning Source LLC
Chambersburg PA
CBHW070351130626
46556CB00007B/3123